This book belongs to

....

www.makebelieveideas.com

Written by Rosie Greening.
Illustrated by Clare Fennell.

We Three Kings

Rosie Greening · Clare Fennell

make
believe
ideas

Long ago, on a special night,
a star was shining clear and bright.
It glowed to show three kings the way

to see a baby, born that day.

King Henry, Fred and Little Abe
had gifts to give the newborn babe:
some frankincense and myrrh to smell,
and blocks of gleaming gold, as well!

Before too long, they reached a land
with **giant** dunes of golden sand.
"Let's all **roll** down!"
King Henry cried.
And so the kings began to slide!

Down the dunes, the three kings rolled 'til Henry said,

"I've lost my *gold!*"

He looked around, but searched in vain –
the golden hills all looked the same!

All seemed lost, but very soon a rattlesnake slid down a dune. "Gold is nice to see," he hissed, "but rattles make a better gift."

He gave his rattles to the kings.

King Henry said, "They're just the thing!

These rattles make a lovely noise –

the baby's sure to love these toys!"

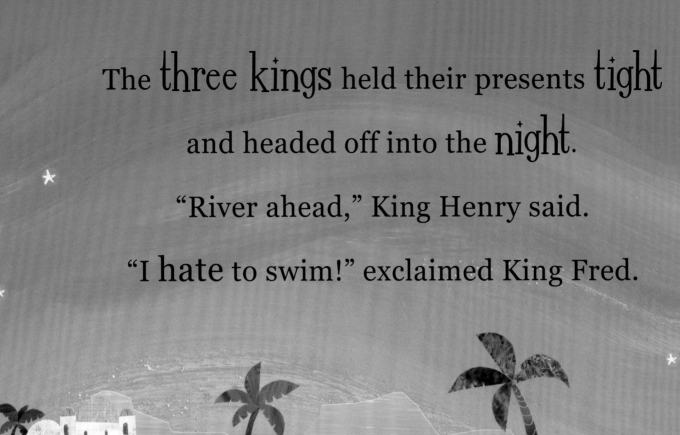

The three kings held their presents tight
and headed off into the night.

"River ahead," King Henry said.

"I hate to swim!" exclaimed King Fred.

The river was both deep and wide,
with waves that crashed on either side.

There was no choice, they dived right in.

And then the kings began to swim.

Before the **three** knew where they were,

they heard Fred **cry**,

"I've dropped my myrrh!"

It sank down to the riverbed,

just out of reach for
poor King Fred.

Fred was just about to cry,
but then a shoal of fish swam by.

"No need to cry! Forget your myrrh.
We've got a gift you might prefer . . ."

The fish brought **shells** for Fred to hold,
of silver, pink and shining gold.

They hung them on some **silky** thread –
a **mobile** for the baby's **bed!**

Fred was thrilled and thanked the fish.

The gift fulfilled his every wish!

And so the kings went on their way

to where the newborn baby lay.

They walked for miles, by starlight led,

until a forest loomed ahead.

By then, it was too dark to see

just where the forest path might be.

Poor little Abe

tripped on a rock

and dropped his frankincense

in shock!

"I've lost my gift!"

King Abe cried out.

"It's gone for good, without a doubt!"

But just as Abe had lost all hope,
some spiders fell from silver rope.

"Frankincense smells nice," they said,
"but why not try our gift instead?"

The spiders used their rope to sew
a blanket made from head to toe
of flowers, buds and leaves of green:
the sweetest gift the kings had seen!

Abe loved the gift, and so the kings
set off with all their brand-new things.
Then all at once the star shone bright
and bathed a stable in its light.

All three kings looked up and smiled.

This was where they'd find the child!

They crept inside, and there He lay

upon a manger full of hay.

The stable wasn't very bright,

with just one candle's glowing light.

The kings all bowed upon one knee

and whispered very quietly . . .

"We three kings come on this day,
to bring you gifts from far away:

presents from the trees and sands,
from rivers and exotic lands."

As Henry, Fred and Little Abe
laid down their presents by the babe,
the unique gifts shone through the gloom
and warmed each heart inside the room.

Soon, the three went on their way.

But now, each year on Christmas Day

we gladly celebrate and sing

about the gifts brought by the kings.

The end.